For Ava Mae, Arthika, Bezawit, Brendan, Carla & Francis, Christine, Edison &
Zewdia, Freya & Rudy, Frederick, Hugh & Martha, Joanie, Joanna & Jagoda,
Jonathan, Kendra, Lola, Laurel & Natalia, Michael, Natalie, Noah, Olivia,
Rebecca, Sakura, Sebastian, Sinnit, Tessa and all the 'regulars'
at the Sure Start Family Book Group in Acton Library.

Dedicated to Abir for not complaining all the mornings
Sally woke her up early to come to the Book Group,
and to Husain for sharing my cappuccino, A McQ

To Philippa, with love, R B

Published in the UK by
Alanna Books, 46 Chalvey Road East,
Slough, Berkshire SL1 2LR, United Kingdom
www.alannabooks.com

First published in hardcover in 2006.
Text copyright © 2006 Anna McQuinn
Illustrations copyright © 2006 Rosalind Beardshaw
Lulu loves the Library copyright © 2006 Alanna Books
This edition published 2016.

ISBN: Hardcover & CD: 978-1-907825-071
Paperback & CD: 978-0-9551998-20
Printed and bound in China

Because
everyone loves
a good story...

Alanna Books

Lulu loves the Library

Anna McQuinn

Illustrated by Rosalind Beardshaw

ALANNA BOOKS

Lulu loves Tuesdays.
On Tuesdays, Lulu and her
mummy go to the library.

The library opens at nine o'clock
but Lulu is ready to go
long before that!

She puts all the books she borrowed
last week in her rucksack.

Her library card is also VERY important.

The library is not very
far away, so Lulu and
her mummy always walk there.

Lulu and her mummy give back the books from last week. The librarian buzzes them through her machine.

There's a special section in the library just for children.

It's really cool and nobody ever says, "shhh!"

Sometimes they even have singing.

Lulu knows all the words
AND the actions for
"Twinkle, Twinkle, Little Star."

Sometimes they have storytime.
Lulu loves that.

After storytime, Lulu chooses
her books. In the library,
she can have ANY book she wants.

Lulu likes stories with bears
and ANYTHING with shoes.
There are so many,
it takes ages to choose!

Mummy has some books, too.
The librarian buzzes them
through the machine,
then stamps the date inside.

Lulu must bring them
back in two weeks,
but she will probably be back
for more long before then!

Lulu and her mummy always go for
a coffee after visiting the library.
Mummy has a cappuccino
and Lulu has juice.

Whenever Lulu has been good, her mummy
lets her taste the froth - mmmmm!

Then it's time to go home again.

Every night, when Lulu is tucked up in bed
her mummy reads her a story.
Sometimes it's nice to read a new story...

but sometimes an old favourite
is the best way to end the day.

Celebrating 10 years of Lulu...

Lulu Loves the Library was published in March 2006, so will be 10 years in print in 2016! Over these 10 years everybody has fallen in love with this pint-size, book-loving hero – critics, journalists, teachers, librarians, booksellers, parents and especially young children. They like how she and her family love books and stories and the way they inspire Lulu's play and imagination – whatever she does in life, Lulu consults a book!

The series has been praised for being 'naturally inclusive' – Lulu doesn't need a reason to be a star in her own story! This combination of warm, child-friendly, inclusive stories, simple text and utterly charming illustrations has made Lulu a huge success. Published in the UK, USA, Netherlands, Denmark, Brazil and Korea, and sold around the world, sales have reached over 300,000.

With a free Multi-language CD

Two of the Lulu titles are accompanied by a Multi-language CD - Listen to the story told in English and over 20 other languages - a perfect resource for inclusive storytimes. Recommended by Book Trust.

Languages: English, Irish, Welsh, French, Dutch, Polish, Spanish, Italian, Portuguese, Turkish, Arabic, Somali, Igbo, Luganda, Swahili, Amharic, Tigrinya, Ndebele, Urdu, Gujarati, Japanese and Chinese.

Look out for Lulu's baby brother, Zeki -now with his own series of adventures!

Zeki and his friends sing familiar favourites - young readres will love to see their everyday world of a visit to the library for rhymetime in a story.

"This brilliant and empowering book... perfectly reflects a baby's life, is warmly drawn, diverse, inclusive and just lovely. A must have for every nursery and playgroup." – Zoe Toft, Playing by the Book

"Books of the Year 2014! A copy should be given to all new parents." – Books for Keeps

ISBN 978-1-907825-101 • 24 toddler-friendly and robust card pages • £7.99 • For age 1 and up

Zeki and his dad meet their friends at swimming class. They learn how to get safely into the water, then off they go - Kick! Kick! Kick! They swish and swoosh, splish and sploosh and even sing a splashy song! Wonderful art and simple text will inspire toddlers everywhere!

Sneak preview - published June 2016 - ISBN 978-1-907825-132 • 24 toddler-friendly and robust card pages • £7.99 • For age 1 and up

www.alannabooks.com

Everyone's favourite pint-sized book lover!

Lulu loves Tuesdays. That's when she and her mummy go to the library. Lulu goes to story time and singing time. Then she chooses books for her mummy to read at bedtime.

"A joyful exploration of books, libraries and sharing stories - this should be available in every library and children's centre." – Annie Everall OBE, Children's Librarian

"Lulu should be mandatory reading for anyone who doubts the impact libraries have on young lives." Liz Broekmann, CYP, SLough Library

Paperback & Free multi-language CD ISBN 978-0-9551998-20 £8.99 – Listen to the story told in over 20 languages - perfect for inclusive storytimes For ages 3 and up
Hardcover & multi-language CD ISBN 978-1-907825-071 £12.99 For ages 3 and up • Board book with shorter, simpler text ISBN 978-0-9551998-75 £4.99 For 6 months & up

Lulu loves stories - each night she reads a different one, and next day she is a fairy, a pilot, a farmer, a mummy, a tiger and a monster!

"An excellent jumping off point for so many reading activities. Having read the story, children will enjoy finding books about princesses, pilots, farmers, friendship, builders and especially 'wild and wicked monsters' for themselves." – Teaching with Picture Books

Paperback & Free multi-language CD ISBN 978-1-907825-019 £8.99 – Listen to the story told in over 20 languages - perfect for inclusive storytimes For ages 3 and up
Hardcover ISBN 978-0-9551998-51 £9.99 For ages 3 and up • Board book with shorter, simpler text ISBN 978-1-907825-002 £4.99 For 6 months and up

From bath time to nap time, Lulu knows just the right story to read to new baby Zeki.

"The roots of reading, along with matters of love and life, are happily married in this bright, uplifting, outstanding and important offering." – School Library Journal

"Excellent. This will be at the top of my list for recommending from the 'new baby' genre. Great addition to the series and stands alone well, too." – Goodreads

Paperback ISBN 978-1-907825-057 £6.99 • Hardcover ISBN 978-1-907825-040 £11.99 • For ages 3 and up

Inspired by a poem she reads, Lulu wants her own garden. She researches, plants her seeds, weeds and hoes, then adds some shells and silver bells until her garden is just fabulous.

"...perfect in every way. That's all you really need to know. It's that simple." – Zoe Toft

Books for Keeps: Book of the Week March 2015 • Reading is Fundamental 2015 Multicultural Book Selection
The NATURE Generation: 2015 Green Earth Book Award • American Booksellers Association: ABC Best Books

Paperback ISBN 978-1-907825-125 £6.99 • Hardcover ISBN 978-1-907825-118   £11.99 • For ages 3 and up

Lulu really really wants a cat. But before Mummy will allow it, Lulu has to prove she's ready for the responsibility. So, she reads up on how to care for a cat and practices on her toy. Once Mummy is convinced, off they go to the cat shelter for a real one. Follow Lulu as she helps her new friend to settle in to her new home. Utterly charming.

Sneak preview - this story is not yet published. Hardcover ISBN 978-1-907825-163 £11.99 • For ages 3 and up

Alanna Books... because everyone loves a good story

Anna McQuinn works part time as a community librarian – the group photographed here are regulars at the Tuesday Family Book Club. Many of the children speak a language different from English at home, so Anna chooses books where the pictures tell the story and can be understood by the whole group. She also encourages the parents to tell the stories in their home language while looking at the pictures in the English edition. Out of this work came the idea of recording the parents telling *Lulu Loves the Library* in their first language – we hope you enjoy the CD whatever language you speak!

Parents:

If you and your child speak English as a first language, you can listen to the story in English. It is also fascinating to listen to some of the story in other languages – listen out for words you know, or work out the word for *mummy* or *story*...

If you speak one of the other languages, you can listen to that version as you and your child look at the pictures together.

Early Years and Speech & Language Professionals:

Using their first language at home supports children's language development. You can use this book & CD to encourage parents and it can be a bridge between home and other settings. If you work in a nursery or play-group or you run a story time attended by children who speak different home languages, you can play the appropriate one to a small group or use it one-to-one with a child. You can even have it playing in the background while you do other non-verbal activities.

If your setting lends books to parents, this CD, with so many different languages, is a great resource and is especially useful where a parent speaks but does not read in their first language. It's also great for grandparents. Enjoy!

Languages on the CD:

1. Introduction
2. English – Mike from England
3. Welsh – Gwen from Wales
4. Irish/Gaeilge – Áine from Ireland
5. French – Blandine from France
6. Dutch – Marijn from Netherlands

7. Polish – Iwona from Poland
8. Italian – Isabella from Italy
9. Turkish – Darya from Turkey
10. Spanish – Jasbet from Mexico
11. Portuguese – Rose from Brasil
12. Arabic - Nada from Eqypt

13. Mandarin – Lingling from China
14. Japanese – Yumiko from Japan
15. Igbo – Alexander from Nigeria
16. Somali – Ayan from Somalia
17. Amharic – Yewbdar from Ethiopia
18. Luganda – Marie from Uganda

19. Swahili – Alpha from Tanzania
20. Ndebele – Gus from Zimbabwe
21. Tigrinya – Weini from Eritrea
22. Urdu – Najma from Pakistan
23. Gujarati – Josh from India
24. Twinkle, Twinkle, Little Star